A Twiggyleaf Adventure

WHAT'S THE HURRY, FURRY?

By Carol Goodwin
Illustrated By Thomas McDaniel

For Lee and Chris
-Carol
For Tom and Joyce
-Thomas

Published By

2635 Whitehall Court   Rock Hill, South Carolina 29732   www.cornerwind.com

Printed in the United States of America
by Jostens, Charlotte, NC
First Edition

ISBN 0-9741072-0-4
Library of Congress Control Number: 2003094750

Please visit

www.Twiggyleaf.com

For Emily Morabito

Always Enjoy Reading!

Carol Goodwin
2004

WELCOME TO THE
TALL PINE WOOD

Thomas McBrian
2004

One beautiful day in the Tall Pine Wood,
as Twiggyleaf lazied around,
he spotted something very far away,
that looked like a rabbit abound.

It jumped so high,
   so high in the sky,
      it looked just like a small cloud
         floating around.

It hopped over that rock.

It came around that tree.

Still so far away,

Twiggyleaf could hardly see.

That rabbit is so silly
there is no doubt.
What could such hopping
be all about?

Over the hill and
through the tall grass,

"I still see him coming,
he is coming real fast."

When closer he came, Twiggyleaf said,
"Why, that's my friend," and called him by name.

"I really must know, I really must say,
What's the hurry, Furry, on this beautiful day?"

6

Furry said to Twiggyleaf,
"What's the hurry you say?"

"Why a wonderful thing will happen today."

"I am in a big hurry,
I really can't stay.
If you want to come with me,
that would be okay."

"But we need to go quickly,
we need to go fast.
We don't want to miss it.
Let's hope it's not past."

Twiggyleaf saw the joy
on Furry's face.
He took off behind him
like the start of a race!

Over roots and bramble
in the bright sunny light,
they went over the creek
down the path on the right.

"It's not too far now," said Furry over his shoulder.
"It should be right around this big boulder."

Just as they came around the big rock,
Furry suddenly came to a very quick stop.
He pointed ahead to a nice little tree.
He said to Twiggyleaf, "There it is, do you see?"

Twiggyleaf said to Furry,

"Do you mean to tell me,
do you mean to say,
that we ran so very fast,
and we ran all that way,"

"Only to see
what I think that I see,
a little piece of cotton
stuck in a tree?"

"Why that's not cotton,
   my dear Twiggyleaf,
      that's not what we came to see.
         Today is the day a new life will be free!"

16

"Oh no, Twiggyleaf,
that's no ordinary piece of fluff.
Last fall a caterpillar worked hard
spinning that silky stuff."

Just then Twiggyleaf
saw what Furry brought him to see,
a tiny new life coming to be.

18

For then the cocoon came apart,
and what appeared
warmed Twiggyleaf's heart.

"Look, Twiggyleaf,
it is a sight to behold.
Look at those colors,
so bright and so bold."

"Oh Furry, I am so happy
I came here today,
to meet a new friend,
What's her name, will she say?"

"Hello, my name is Flitter.
I am a butterfly you see.
I am as happy to see you
as you are to see me."

22

"Will you show me around
to see all the sights?
Will you be my friends,
both day and night?"

Twiggyleaf and Furry
with smiles on their faces
said, "Of course we'll be friends
and show you great places."

"Come along with us now,
you can ride the light breeze,
and gaze at the sights
from the tops of the trees."

So they set out

through the Tall Pine Wood

to show Flitter their home

which is so very good.

It was a wonderful day to make
a new friend,
and because it's a beginning,
it's not really…
THE END.

See ya!